D0417771

With special thanks to Tabitha Jones

For Tom Oliver Duncan Gater –
the most inspirational person I've met

www.seaquestbooks.co.uk

ORCHARD BOOKS
Carmelite House
50 Victoria Embankment
London EC4Y 0DZ

A Paperback Original
First published in Great Britain in 2015

Series created by Beast Quest Limited, London

Text © Beast Quest Limited 2015
Cover and inside illustrations by Artful Doodlers, with special thanks
to Bob and Justin © Orchard Books 2015

A CIP catalogue record for this book is available from
the British Library.

ISBN 978 1 40833 469 0

1 3 5 7 9 10 8 6 4 2

Printed and bound by CPI Group (UK) Ltd, Croydon, CR0 4YY

MIX
Paper from
responsible sources
FSC® C104740

The paper and board used in this book are made from wood from
responsible sources.

Orchard Books
An imprint of Hachette Children's Group
Part of The Watts Publishing Group Limited
An Hachette UK Company

www.hachette.co.uk

JANDOR
THE ARCTIC LIZARD

BY ADAM BLADE

ORCHARD

> OCEANS OF NEMOS:
  THE FROZEN NORTH

> TRANSMISSION

FROM: CORA BLACKHEART

TO: COUNCILLOR REGULIS

Look alive, Regulis! I'm coming
aboard. I want my crew swabbing
the decks and sharpening their
hyperblades. We set sail in one hour.

Finally everything is ready... Jandor
is waiting, locked in its prison of
ice. And once we've stolen the Arms
of Addulis from the worthless Merryn,
we'll set the Beast free...

I can't wait to see the look on Max's
face when we destroy his city, and
Sumara too. Be afraid, boy, wherever
you are. Jandor the Arctic Lizard is
coming for you!

> END TRANSMISSION

STORY 1:

THE EYE OF THALLOS

CHAPTER ONE

GILL POX

Max stared up at the coral ceiling, trying not to wriggle, while Tarla examined the gills on either side of his neck. The gentle touch of the Merryn healer's webbed fingers tickled like mad, and his nose was starting to itch too. *Lia will never let me hear the end of it if I sneeze in Tarla's face*, he thought.

To distract himself, he shifted his gaze to the potions and boxes that lined the coral walls. *I hope Tarla's got something to help me,* he thought. His body had never ached so badly, and the doctors back home in Aquora had no idea what was wrong with him.

Tarla stood back and smoothed down the folds of her turquoise robe. "Well, I think we can safely say you'll survive," she said, smiling. "You have a standard case of gill pox."

From her place at the side of his bed, Lia let out a burst of laughter. "Gill pox?" she said. "Is that all? From the way you were going on I'd expected at least the creeping rot! I had gill pox when I was little and I didn't even get a day off school."

Max flipped himself up on the clamshell bed. The movement made his head pound, and he scowled at Lia. "Well, maybe it's worse in humans," he said. "After all, we're not even supposed to have gills. In a way this is your fault for giving me the Merryn Touch."

Lia rolled her eyes. "Clearly," she said, "because if I hadn't, you'd have drowned long ago and wouldn't be here to get sick!"

"Hush, Lia," Tarla said, before turning back to Max. "I dare say you're right, Max. Gill pox is probably much worse for humans."

Max shot Lia a look of triumph, only to find that she and Tarla were already exchanging a smile, their eyes glinting with amusement.

"Well, I'm glad you're both finding this so hilarious," Max said, "but have you got anything to help me feel better?"

"You need rest," Tarla said, "and one strand of sourweed four times a day." Her bright robe billowed as she swam to a table on the other side of the room and opened a small shell box. She took a handful of seaweed strands from the box, and packed them into a pouch. "This should take the edge off things until your body fights the infection,"

she said, handing the pouch to Max. "But
don't take more than one strand at a time or
you'll feel very groggy."

Max opened the bag and grimaced at the
smell. It was like a cross between vinegar
and old socks. He popped a strand into his
mouth and swallowed it quickly.

"Ugh!" he said, shuddering at the taste.

"Does tinkering in the tech graveyard count as rest? Because I've got a bike I'm working on and..." Tarla's expression turned very stern and Max trailed off.

"Rest means rest!" Tarla said. "The last thing you should be doing with a headful of sourweed is playing with dangerous tech!"

Max's spirits sank. *Not only am I sick, but now I have to lie around doing nothing all day!*

Tarla must have noticed his gloom, because her expression softened. "Don't worry – you'll be back to full health in no time."

Max sighed. "Here, Riv!" he said, beckoning his dogbot, Rivet, from the side of the bed.

Rivet swam over and licked Max's hand. "Rivet look after Max!" the dogbot barked.

"Thanks, Rivet," Max said, putting his pouch of sourweed into Rivet's back compartment. "At least someone knows how to show sympathy."

Max waved goodbye to Tarla and swam out into the softly lit waters of Sumara, followed by Rivet and Lia. The street was busy with Merryn men and women riding swordfish and swimming between brightly coloured coral towers and arches. Lia's pet swordfish, Spike, was waiting for them, and Lia slid onto his back. They set off at a leisurely pace, drifting past the sparkling rock buildings that made up the Merryn city.

Once Tarla's hut was well out of sight, Max turned towards the tech graveyard on the outskirts of town.

"Hey!" Lia said. "I thought you were going to rest."

"But I feel so much better after taking that sourweed," Max lied. "And I've got something I want to show you."

Lia rolled her eyes, but she kept pace with Max as he headed down the craggy ocean trench that led away from the city.

Before long, the trench opened up to reveal a wide plain, scattered with shadowy piles of broken subs and sunken ships. The tech graveyard was a resting place for all the technology the Merryn people had salvaged from the ocean. It was also Max's personal workshop. Max lifted his new communicator wristwatch to his mouth.

"Sleekfin, come," he said. There was a low thrum, and moments later, what looked like a large shiny swordfish with handlebars and a windscreen zoomed towards them from behind a pile of debris. Its body was made from interlocking metal plates, and its huge eyes cast long beams of light through the water. "High-powered LEDs," Max said as Lia shielded her eyes.

His newest invention slid to a stop just before them, tail whipping from side to

side. Lia's expression was hard to read, but Max thought she looked pretty amazed – or possibly horrified. Spike backed away, eyeing the bike warily. Only Rivet seemed completely at ease with Max's new invention. He darted towards it, barking excitedly.

"Okay," Lia said, finally, "I don't know whether to be more impressed or creeped out by that thing. You've clearly taken inspiration

from the sea, which is good. But given your uncle's obsession with creating deadly Robobeasts, do you really think you should be heading down that path?"

Max chuckled. "It's just a bike," he said. "But it does have some pretty advanced features." He swam onto the padded seat on the metal swordfish's back, and spun the bike around to face Lia. "Its eyes emit normal light," he said, "but also infrared and UV. That means I'll be able to see in almost any light conditions – and detect creatures by their body heat!" Max flicked a switch, and Sleekfin's eyes flashed brightly for a moment. "It can even take Ultra-Scans," Max said, turning his bike so Lia could see the watershield, which also acted as a viewing screen. He loaded the snap he'd just taken.

Lia grimaced at the sight of her own skeleton, perched upon Spike's transparent form, his ribs and vertebrae seeming to float beneath her. "Nice," she said flatly. "I'm sure being able to see your enemy's insides will be very useful in a battle."

Max grinned. "It's got weapons as well, obviously." He hit a button, and felt the bike vibrate as the torpedo launcher lowered from its underbelly. Then he toggled a joystick with his thumb, aiming his side-fin blasters.

BOOM! Max jolted upright in surprise. It wasn't his bike firing – he hadn't even hit the trigger. But he could hear shouts of alarm and blaster fire drifting towards them on the current. He and Lia turned towards Sumara. Bright red bursts of energy lit up the ocean at the heart of the city.

Adrenaline surged through Max. "Sumara's under attack!" he cried.

CHAPTER TWO

DEADLY SEAWEED

Sleekfin's engines roared as Max turned the throttle and shot forwards, with Lia and Spike at his side. Rivet whizzed ahead as they raced back along the deep-sea trench towards Sumara.

They burst from the dark crevasse to find the elegant spires of the Merryn city overshadowed by the curved underbelly of an enormous timber-hulled sub. The sub was drifting over Sumara's busy main square,

scores of armed divers pouring from an
open airlock in its side. The divers were all
wearing breathing masks and grey deepsuits,
with what looked like a black skull-and-
crossbones on their chests. Blasts of red
energy rained down on the city from the
attacking divers, while the Merryn citizens
below fled for shelter.

"Pirates, Max!" Rivet barked.

Max revved Sleekfin's engines, trying to get

more speed out of his new bike as he raced towards the square. Beside him, Lia lifted her spear.

"They're going to destroy the statue of Thallos!" Lia cried.

Sure enough, the pirate divers were all aiming their blasters down towards the huge sacred sea creature carved from stone.

Merryn warriors quickly surrounded the statue, throwing up their coral shields to deflect the blasts, and launching harpoons at the swarming pirates. But energy bullets were falling thick and fast as more grey-clad attackers dived into the square.

"Cora Blackheart must be behind this," Max called to Lia, drawing his hyperblade. "But why would she attack a statue? It doesn't make any sense!"

"I don't know," Lia called back, "but we have to stop them!"

"I'll go and block the pirates leaving the ship," Max said. 'You help in the square. Rivet, you stay with Lia." Lia nodded and she and Rivet darted away. Max steered Sleekfin upwards towards the hovering ship, aiming his side-fin blasters as he went. *Time to find out what Sleekfin can do!*

BAM BAM BAM! Max shot a hail of blaster fire at a pair of pirates emerging from the hull. One clutched his shoulder and started swimming back towards the ship. The other flailed in panic, his breathing tube severed, before following his friend through the airlock. Max fired again, straight for the airlock itself. The door slid shut and his blaster fire ricocheted off the hull.

Max swerved and dived downwards to join Lia and Rivet in the square. The Merryn soldiers around the statue of Thallos had locked their shields together, creating a barricade. They jabbed at their attackers with long lances, while Rivet snapped and Lia zoomed about on Spike, dodging the pirates' fire and stabbing with her spear.

Max steered Sleekfin towards a grey-clad form. But as he took aim, he found himself struggling to focus, his hands shaking. The sourweed must be wearing off, he realised. He hit *fire*, but his shot went wide. The pirate spun in the water and grinned, revealing black stumps of teeth, then lifted his blaster. Max steered sharply away, but felt a jolt as an energy bolt glanced off Sleekfin's bumper. Water swirled past him and his stomach lurched as the bike went into a downwards spin. Max tried to cling on, but his arms were heavy, and the whirling current tugged him from Sleekfin's back as the bike spiralled away.

Max righted himself, and lifted his watch to his lips. "Sleekfin, come!" he said. His bike swerved upwards and came to a halt in the water before him. As Max climbed back on, he glanced towards the pirate sub above.

The hatch was still closed, but as Max watched, another airlock near the front of the ship slid open, and two dark forms, one powerfully built and one slim, slipped out. The divers started swimming between the Merryn buildings towards the palace, darting

from shadow to shadow as they went. *What are they after in the palace?* Max wondered.

"Lia!" Max called into his headset. "Pirates are heading towards the palace. We have to warn the king!" Max scanned the chaos in the square, and spotted Lia darting forward on Spike, swiping her spear at a pirate with an enormous belly. The butt of the spear smashed into the side of the pirate's head, knocking him unconscious. Spike turned, carrying Lia towards Max. Rivet appeared behind her, spitting a bit of ragged grey material from between his metal teeth.

"They went that way!" Max said, pointing towards the coral towers of the palace. His finger wavered as he pointed, and a shudder of sickness ran through his body. Max flipped Rivet's back compartment open, and took another strand of sourweed to swallow. Gradually he felt the chill of his fever recede and his strength coming back. The weed seemed to be working faster as his body got used to it.

"Okay, Max?" Rivet barked.

Max nodded. "Fine now, Riv. Come on." He twisted the throttle and surged forwards, Lia at his side. Together, they raced towards the palace entrance. They swooped through the coral arch and down the corridor that led to the throne room, then burst through the fronds of weed that covered the door.

Max scanned the huge room, running his eyes over the pearl throne, high arched windows and towering columns. There was no one there.

"Father must have gone to defend the city," Lia said. "But where are the pirates?"

Max turned a dial on his bike's dashboard, switching his headlamps to infrared. The lights appeared to go out, but Max could see a wavering orange trail in the water, showing where something or someone warm had recently passed.

"Glowing, Max," Rivet said, sniffing at the shimmering streak.

"They went that way," Max told Lia, pointing to a low side door.

"The treasure vaults," Lia said.

"That makes sense," Max said. "Pirates love booty. The attack on the statue must have been a decoy."

"Well, they won't get far," Lia said. "The vaults are protected by kelp."

"Kelp!" Max almost laughed despite his worry. "How's a bunch of seaweed going to stop armed pirates?"

Lia grinned. "It's flesh-eating kelp," she said, "and if they manage to get through it alive, which they won't, there's a thick stone door."

"What are we waiting for, then?" Max said. "If they do make it through, they'll be trapped!"

Lia looked worried for a moment, then nodded. She slipped from Spike's back. "Spike, go and find Father," she told her swordfish. "Tell him we have intruders heading to the vaults." Lia's pet lifted his sword in agreement, then swam away.

"Follow pirates, Max?" Rivet barked, his nose twitching and his tail wagging as he sniffed at their infrared trail.

Max revved his bike, accelerating forward. "That's right, Rivet. Full speed ahead."

"Not so fast!" Lia cried. "I told you. The kelp in that corridor's deadly!"

Max pulled his bike to a stop outside the low arch. "So how do we get through?" he asked.

"You have to sing a song that only a very few of the most trusted Merryn know," Lia said.

"But you know it, right?" Max asked.

"Yeees…" Lia said. "Or most of it, anyway. I heard my father singing it once."

"Once?" A twinge of fear stirred in Max's stomach. "Well, I suppose that will just have to be enough," he said, moving his bike away from the door so that Lia could lead him inside.

The corridor was narrower and dimmer than Max had expected. As he and Rivet followed Lia into the half-darkness, Max saw red strands rising up from the coral floor covered in tiny round blisters. It doesn't look that deadly…

"Ouch!" Something snagged Max's leg, slicing through the fabric of his wetsuit and circling his ankle with a searing pain. He jerked his leg upwards, snatching it free of a clutching frond. Through the rip in his

suit he could see a ring of circular welts all around his ankle.

"Bad plants!" Rivet barked, snapping at the fronds.

Max rubbed at the painful marks on his ankle, and glanced at the swaying coils of weed. "I don't see any sign of those pirates," he said, his voice hoarse. "Do you think they could have been eaten already?"

Lia shook her head. "The kelp couldn't digest two whole people that fast."

Max's skin tightened with a sudden chill as he peered into the gloom. The whole tunnel ahead, ceiling, walls and floor, was covered in the red-tentacled kelp, and as he watched, it stopped swaying gently and unfurled, reaching long fronds towards him.

"Hungry seaweed," Rivet barked.

Max leaned closer to Lia. "Um…maybe it's time to start singing that song?" he hissed.

Lia nodded, and began to sing a soft, wavering tune. Max noticed with relief that the kelp responded immediately, sagging gently towards the floor or hanging limply downwards. Lia waved with her hand for Max and Rivet to follow, and swam ahead, still singing.

Max clung tightly to his bike, barely daring to breathe. His ankle was burning like he'd been stung by a jellyfish, and he couldn't help imagining what it would feel like to be slowly eaten alive by a plant. He edged closer to Lia as she sang. Up ahead, the corridor widened into a bare cavern with a round stone door set into the floor. Almost there…

Suddenly Lia stopped singing and turned to Max, biting her lip.

"What?" Max said.

"I don't know any more of the song," she said, her voice quavering. Her eyes looked enormous in the dark, as the red tentacles all around them twitched. Before Max could hit the accelerators, strands of weed covered with suckers lashed towards him from all directions, grabbing hold of the bike. Max revved Sleekfin's engines, his pulse thrashing in his ears. It wouldn't budge!

Max heard Rivet's propellers whir as the dogbot cannoned into Sleekfin, throwing Max and his bike through the tunnel of weed. Fronds snapped around Max as he hurtled past, gripping desperately to the handlebars. The bike spun, out of control. Crack! Sleekfin's front bumper hit the wall of the cavern at the end with a thud. Max just managed to stay seated, and spun his bike around.

Now Rivet was shoving Lia with his powerful, blunt nose, throwing her through the twisting arms of the kelp into the safety of the cavern.

"Keep going, boy!" Max called.

Rivet powered after Lia, but then let out a yelp. Max's scalp tingled with horror as he saw a red lasso of weed wrapped around the dogbot's back paw. Rivet's thrusters squealed as he tried to pull free of the weed, but more

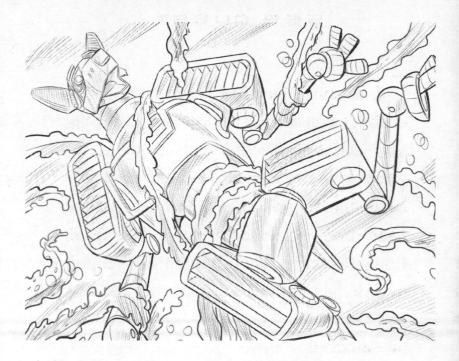

fronds wrapped around his body and neck.

Rivet howled as they pulled him down to the tunnel floor. "Help, Max!" In an instant, the dogbot had disappeared inside a red cocoon of matted fronds.

Max drew his hyperblade and dived forwards, but Lia grabbed his arm. "I have to help him!" Max cried.

"No!" she said firmly. "It will kill you!" Max struggled in her grip, but the weed was reaching hungrily towards him. Lia was right. Max felt a hollow sickness in his stomach. *Rivet! No!* But as he watched, the coils of weed started to loosen their grip on the dogbot, writhing angrily. A moment later, Rivet powered out of the mass of lashing tentacles. He shook himself all over as he joined them beside the door.

"Nasty plants, Max!" Rivet said.

"You're right there!" Max said, his heart thumping with relief. "Lucky they don't seem to like the taste of dogbot." He patted Rivet's head, then glanced around the shadowy chamber. "So, where have those pirates got to?" He turned his attention to the circular door in the floor of the cavern. "Does that lead to the vaults?" he asked Lia.

It was a solid-looking slab of stone, encrusted with barnacles which partly covered the swirling lines of ancient runes.

In the centre of the door was a keyhole.

"Yup," Lia said. "But even if someone had made it this far, they couldn't have passed through the door without a key. Maybe they turned back. Or never came this way to begin with."

"Wrong!" A nasal voice spoke from above. Two figures in grey deepsuits swam from behind a rocky outcrop in the roof of the cavern, aiming their blasters at Max and Lia. The one who'd spoken was a Merryn, and Max recognised him at once. Regulis! A treacherous former councillor, he had been banished from Sumara in disgrace.

He's disguised himself as a pirate, Max realised. Regulis's companion wore a breathing mask and had a robotic leg. Long black hair flowed around her angular face, and her dark eyes glinted. Cora Blackheart. Max clenched his fists in anger. *This explains*

a lot. Regulis would have known the song to calm the kelp!

"I had hoped you'd got the message to stay away for good!" Lia said, glaring at the Merryn traitor.

Regulis shrugged his shoulders. "And why would I do that?" he said. "It's still high time Sumara had a new leader. I was just lying low until I could find a new ally."

Cora darted in front of Regulis.

"Shut your trap, will you?" she said. "I've got no interest in Merryn politics. I've come here for my prize. And you're just in time to see me claim it. The Arms of Addulis are mine!"

CHAPTER THREE
BREAKING THE VAULT

Max gripped the hilt of his hyperblade. *Of course – it all makes sense now! The Arms of Addulis, the most powerful battle gear in the ocean, are stored in the palace vaults.* "We have to stop Cora getting in there!" he said to Lia. He started to draw his blade, but Cora grinned back at him, her finger on the trigger of her blaster. Meanwhile Regulis aimed his weapon at Lia.

"I wouldn't make any fast movements if I

were you," Cora said. "There's nothing you can do to stop me now."

Lia shrugged. "We can't stop you getting into the vaults, but that stone door definitely can. Only my father has the key. So you're not getting anywhere near the Arms of Addulis."

Cora laughed. "Oh, I think Regulis will be able to open the door."

Regulis's thin lips spread into a smarmy grin. Max found himself itching to wipe the smile off the traitor's face, but with Cora's blaster aimed at his chest, that would have to wait.

"Does this look familiar?" Regulis said, drawing a whalebone key from his pocket. He shot Lia a look of triumph. "I had your father's key copied long ago," he said.

Lia said nothing as the traitor swam down to the cavern floor and slotted the key into the ornate keyhole. He gave it a twist, but it didn't turn. Regulis yanked at the key, but it still didn't budge. Max could see Cora's jaw flexing under her mask as she balled her fists and glared at the disgraced official.

Regulis revealed his white teeth in a nervous smile. "Er...there seems to be a problem with the door," he said.

Lia grinned. "Father changed the locks after the last time you betrayed the city. He might have been kind enough to spare your life, but he's not a fool."

Regulis swam away from the door, and cowered against the wall of the cavern. He shook as he met Cora's furious eyes. "I...I...I..." Regulis faltered.

Cora rolled her eyes and waved her hand dismissively. "No matter," she said. "If you want a job done properly..." She plucked a shiny black globe from her belt. It was about the size of an apple, and as she weighed it in her hand, Rivet whined anxiously. "I've got something just as effective as an old key," Cora said, "and a lot more fun. It's called a High Intensity Detonation Device. Or, as I prefer to call it, a bomb!"

Max revved his bike towards Cora, but before he could reach her, Cora lifted her

hand and hurled the ball at the door.

BOOM! A wall of swirling water and broken rock smashed into Max, throwing him backwards off his bike. Sharp coral bit into his back and his head smacked against something hard. Bright lights filled his vision, and he started to fall. When he finally managed to blink the lights away, he found himself sitting on the cavern floor beside his bike. Fragments of stone hung in the water around him.

Lia was lying nearby, with Rivet nudging her gently. Worry flared inside Max, but then his friend sat up, rubbing her eyes. As her gaze fell on the floor of the cavern, she gasped. The stone door was gone, leaving a gaping hole. Cora and Regulis were nowhere to be seen. Max drew his hyperblade and swam towards the dark opening, blinking groggily. He peered inside, and once his eyes

had adjusted to the dim light, his wooziness
vanished with a rush of fear.

The vault was piled high with jewels, coins
and carved statues. Cora was floating in
the centre of the room above the glittering
mounds, wearing the Stone Breastplate
of Addulis. In one hand she held the Pearl
Spear of Strength, and in the other the
Coral Sword. Her dark eyes flashed with
victory as Regulis lifted Addulis's Helmet

and placed it on her head.

No! Max dived through the hole, swinging his hyperblade. Cora's sword arm moved in a blur of magical speed, channelling the quickness of the nimblest fish. *CLASH!* Max's weapon flew from his hand, leaving his arm ringing with pain. Lia darted past him, spear raised. Cora sent the Pearl Spear swishing through the water.

"Ah!" Lia was smashed aside by the shaft, which was magically filled with the power of the strongest ocean creatures. She tumbled over and over before hitting the wall of the vault. Rivet let out a growl and cannoned into Cora's chest, but bounced off, slamming into a wooden chest with a thunk. He shook himself.

"Hard, Max!" Rivet barked.

The Breastplate was magic too, Max knew, as hardy as deep-sea animals who could survive the crushing weight of the water. Cora laughed a long, exultant cackle, then shot upwards in a blur of swirling water, powered by the speed and strength of the Arms of Addulis. She disappeared through the broken roof of the vault into the cavern above.

Max gritted his teeth against the pain engulfing his bruised body, snatched his

hyperblade from a mound of sparkling jewels and swam to Lia's side. "Quick! Before she escapes!" he said.

Lia already had her spear, and with Rivet on their tail, they darted out of the vault after Cora. When they reached the cavern above, they found King Salinus and Spike already there, along with a troop of mounted Merryn warriors, blocking the entrance to

the kelp tunnel and aiming their spears at Cora's chest. Regulis was swimming next to his master, watching her uneasily.

"Put down your weapons, Cora," Salinus commanded. "Your plan has failed. It's over."

"Put down the Arms of Addulis?" Cora said. "Not likely. I think you'll find my plan has only just begun." She nodded her head towards Salinus and his men. The king let out an angry cry as his swordfish bucked him off. Then the other Merryn warriors tumbled from their thrashing mounts, and even Spike started spinning in circles. Max gasped in horror.

The Helmet has given Cora Aqua Powers!

Cora whooped. "Oh! This Helmet is even more fun than I'd hoped," she said. Then she kicked her legs and powered towards the roof of the cavern, lifting the Pearl Spear above her head.

"You said you'd take me with you!" Regulis shrieked, clutching hold of Cora's robotic leg. "You said I was your number two!"

Cora's lips curled into an amused sneer. "For a traitor you're very trusting," she said. "Now I've got what I wanted, why on Nemos would I need a number two?" She shook her metal limb, throwing Regulis off, then thrust the Coral Spear upwards to smash through the rock above her. Fragments of stone clattered down as Cora disappeared, boring a tunnel with the Spear's incredible strength.

"After her!" Max cried.

CHAPTER FOUR

TREACHERY AND BETRAYAL

"**S**pike!" Lia called, but her swordfish was too busy chasing his tail to respond. There was no time to get Sleekfin either.

"Hold onto Rivet," Max said.

They both gripped tight to Rivet's collar. Rivet's thrusters growled, and he motored upwards through the hole in the roof, tugging Max and Lia with him. Water swooshed past as they raced through the narrow tunnel, then

shot out into the open ocean. Max narrowed his eyes against the current, looking for any sign of Cora.

"She's almost reached her sub!" Lia cried, pointing.

Max glanced towards the timber hull hanging over the city and saw the slim, dark form of Cora disappear into the hatch. Only

Merryn warriors remained in the city square now, and as soon as the hatch slid shut, Cora's sub started to rise.

"Follow that ship!" Max told Rivet.

"Got it, Max!" Rivet barked, towing Max and Lia up through the water. Rivet swam so fast that Max's ears popped, but Cora's ship reached the shimmering surface before them. Lia pulled on her Amphibio mask, as Rivet tugged them above the waves into the buffeting wind. Max blinked and glanced about him. Rolling white caps driven by the gale slapped and foamed at his chest, and ragged grey clouds scudded overhead.

Cora's sub was heading towards the horizon, changing shape as it went. Masts draped with rigging rose up from the deck, and huge while sails unfurled as pirates tugged on ropes. Above the mainsail, a black skull-and-crossbones fluttered in the wind.

Cora was already standing at the gunwale, shielding her eyes, and as Max watched, she lifted her hand and waved. Portholes opened all along the side of her ship, and a line of blaster cannons poked out.

"Get down!" Max cried, as a red energy blast arced through the sky and ploughed into the waves nearby. He dived and kicked downwards with Rivet and Lia beside him. He glanced up to see flashes of blaster fire churning the water above him. Once they were deep below the surface, Max turned and squinted into the distance. He could just make out the shadowy shape of the vessel slipping out of sight.

"We can't hope to catch them now!" Lia said.

Max nodded. "So we need to go and question Regulis. We'll find out where Cora's headed, then we'll go and get that armour back!"

o o o

They found Regulis in the throne room in Sumara, kneeling before the king, bound in heavy chains and surrounded by Merryn guards.

Max and Lia took their places at the king's side, while Spike waited with Rivet by the door.

"So what am I to do with my once-loyal councillor this time?" Salinus asked, glaring fiercely at Regulis.

"Bind his mouth shut so he can't sing, and throw him to the kelp!" one of the guards shouted. A murmur of approval ran through the room, but Salinus shook his head.

"We're not savages," he said. "But it will take a long spell in the palace dungeons before I'll even consider letting him out. Regulis? Do you have any words to offer in your defence?"

Regulis attempted a bow, but with his hands chained, it was a clumsy manoeuvre. He swallowed hard as he looked at the king. "I had no choice, Your Majesty," he said. "Cora said she would kill me if I didn't do as she asked."

Lia tutted loudly. "Oh, for Thallos' sake!" she said. "That's the most pathetic excuse

I've ever heard. You could easily have escaped or led her into a trap. The truth is you wanted to join her. You deserve everything you get for letting Cora get hold of Addulis's battle gear. "

"Weapons that will make her practically unstoppable," Max added. "Tell us what Cora's planning while there's still time for us to act."

A sly look crossed Regulis's face as he glanced from Max to Salinus. "I'm not completely sure what she's up to," he said. "She's got some wild idea about making her own Robobeast, but she hasn't got a clue how."

A Robobeast? Max thought. *That's impossible.* He looked at Lia, and she shook her head, clearly thinking the same thing. Max's uncle, the Professor, and his vengeful half-robotic son Siborg were the only ones capable of building robotic beasts.

"She's got a new base," continued Regulis. "That much I do know. I can tell you where it is…' Regulis shot the king a crafty look. "If you'll set me free, that is."

Salinus brought his big fist down hard on the arm of his throne. "You will tell me the location or I will double your sentence," he said. "That is the only offer I am prepared to make. If the information proves reliable, I will consider halving it. So, unless you want to spend the rest of your life rotting in a cell, I suggest you talk now!" Salinus glared at his prisoner, his blue eyes burning with fury.

Regulis scowled, but finally he dropped his eyes, and nodded.

"She's in the north," he said. "Heading for an icy island right below the Eye of Thallos."

"The Eye of Thallos?" Max asked.

"It's what we call the constellation of stars that sits above the northernmost pole of Nemos," Lia said.

"Then we'd better wrap up warm," Max

said. "Cora's got a head start on us already." As he spoke, he felt a shiver rising inside him. He tried to suppress it, but his teeth chattered together, and his knees started to shake. All at once, his head was throbbing and his throat was scratchy and tight. *It's the gill pox again*, he realised.

"I'm afraid I can't send any warriors with you," Salinus said. "I will need them to guard the city in case Cora returns to attack us."

Max nodded, his teeth chattering like clam castanets. Lia frowned.

"But what about your gill pox?" she said. "You're supposed to be resting."

"Yeah, right!" Max said through his shivers. "With Cora on the loose? I just need more of that sourweed. I'll rest when the Arms of Addulis are back where they belong. Now let's go!"

CHAPTER FIVE

THE EYE OF THALLOS

Max sped away from Sumara on Sleekfin, chewing on a fresh strand of sourweed. The chilly water rushing past his fevered gills felt good, and Sleekfin's twin thrusters and streamlined shape meant he could easily keep up with Lia, riding Spike at his side. *I don't know what Tarla was worried about!* Max thought. *This is way better than resting up!*

Rivet zoomed ahead at full throttle, leading

them due north. As they sped towards the pole, the water became deeper and darker, until even Sleekfin's headlamps couldn't penetrate more than a few bike-lengths ahead. The ocean was ice cold too. Max could feel the chill of it even through the fabric of his deepsuit.

"Whoa!" he gasped. A huge, pale fish, glowing with a sickly green light, lurched out of the depths. Its mouth gaped wide, showing uneven, jagged teeth. Max swerved sharply, straight into the middle of a school of jellyfish which pulsed with electric blue lights. He tugged on the controls, scanning the darkness. With a rush of relief, he spotted Rivet's glowing red eyes ahead, and steered towards his friends.

"Let's head up to the surface," Max said. "We must be almost there."

Lia pulled her seaweed jacket tighter

around her. "Agreed," she said.

Max steered his aquabike upwards. The higher they climbed, the colder it seemed, but it wasn't getting any lighter.

When they finally broke the surface, a sudden blast of freezing air seemed to squeeze Max's lungs like a vice. Beside him, Lia tugged on her Amphibio mask, her hands shaking and her teeth chattering. The sky above them was black. There was no moon, but thousands of silver-white stars glimmered in the darkness.

Lia pointed at the northern sky. "The Eye of Thallos," she said.

Max saw a bright star with a bluish tinge gleaming like a beacon. Two smaller stars twinkled on either side. It was a constellation Max knew, but in Aquora they called it the Hub, because the rest of the stars seemed to wheel around it. It was much brighter here than he'd ever seen it before.

Max swept Sleekfin's headlamps over the surface of the water. Pale, shadowy forms rose from the waves, reflecting his beams. Icebergs, Max realised.

"It's not going to be easy to find Cora among these icebergs," he said.

"True," Lia said. "And we've still got a way to go. Let's head back underwater before we freeze. I didn't think it was possible, but it's actually colder up here!"

Max gunned his engines and ducked below the waves. He switched his headlamps to UV, and gasped in wonder as the seascape around him lit up with a purple glow, cast much further ahead than regular light. Icebergs reached up to the surface, shining with an electric blue light, and shoals of pale, silent fish shone like stars in the winter sky. They travelled on in silence, slaloming between

the towering columns of ice. Max could feel the bitter cold creeping into his bones, while his nose was completely numb. Lia was clinging tight to Spike's back, her teeth chattering as they swam, and even Spike gave the occasional shudder. Only Rivet was unaffected by the cold, swimming ahead of them with his tail wagging happily.

Eventually, the ocean began to brighten,

the surface above shining like liquid silver in the morning sun. Max flicked his headlamps to visible light, glad to be rid of the eerie purple glow. Two vast walls of ice closed off the view ahead, and Max steered Sleekfin through a narrow gap between them. Lia followed on Spike.

"Strange," Lia said, as they passed through the pale tunnel. Max glanced back to see her running her fingers over a pattern of furrows in the surface of the ice. "These lines almost look man-made," she said. "As if someone carved the passage."

The tunnel came to an abrupt end, and Max led the others into a widening bay.

Rivet let out a sudden warning growl, as something shadowy and insubstantial rushed upwards to meet Max. "Look out!" Max called. He tried to turn back, but the fibres of a net tightened around him and his

bike. He couldn't move.

Whoosh! Max's stomach leapt as the net tugged him up through the water, and out into freezing sunlight.

CHAPTER SIX

CAUGHT IN A NET

Max blinked, adjusting his eyes to the bright sun. Through the strings of the net that held him, he could see a craggy rock face stretching down to the lapping waves below. He squirmed and twisted, trying to reach the hyperblade at his belt, but he couldn't move his arms. Each time he struggled, a musical jingle rang out around him. He looked up to see a beam protruding from an icy overhang above him, from which the net dangled. A

string of silver bells attached to the beam
sounded as he squirmed.

"Max! Are you okay?" Lia called from
behind her Amphibio mask, her head poking
out of the water below.

"Get down, Max!" Rivet barked.

"I'm fine, but I can't get down!" Max
shouted back.

Lia squinted up at him, shading her eyes
against the sun. She slid from Spike's back.
"Free Max!" she told her swordfish.

Spike dipped his nose and slid under the
water. A moment later, he broke the surface,
flipping himself upwards, sword first. He
dived in a high arc towards the net, but then
plunged back into the sea. When he surfaced
again he clicked and shook his head. He
couldn't reach the net.

"Rivet! You try!" Max called to his dogbot.

"Yes, Max!" Rivet barked. The dogbot's

thrusters roared as he shot out of the water. *Come on, boy!* But Rivet didn't even come close. He landed back in the water with an almighty splash.

"Can't reach, Max!" Rivet barked.

Max twisted his body, trying to get hold of his hyperblade again. The little bells rang and rang, but it was no use. Suddenly, the jingling stopped. Max looked up to see two tall, slim figures with narrow faces and enormous eyes gazing down at him. Their skin glowed the same pale blue as the icebergs under UV, and they were watching Max with a look of distaste on their smooth, fine-featured faces. Max recognised them at once from his last Quest to the north, when he'd fought Nephro the Ice Lobster. *Arctirians!* Beautiful, vain and completely self-obsessed. But at least they weren't evil.

One of the Arctirians turned to the other,

his high forehead barely wrinkling as he
frowned. "What is that vile thing we have
caught in our net?" he asked.

A pained look crossed his companion's face
as he stared down at Max. "I was hoping for
something pretty for our specimen tank," he

said. "But that definitely won't do. I suppose we'd better haul it up anyway."

The two slim creatures started to turn a winch. The net lurched, and Max found himself rising slowly past the cliff face. He glanced down at Lia and Rivet below, and put his fingers to his lips, gesturing for them to stay quiet.

It's probably best if I do the talking for now...

"I'm Max!" he called up to the Arctirians. "Don't you remember me?"

"What's a Max?" one of the Arctirians said to the other. "It looks more like a grubby little Aquoran to me." Together, the two creatures hauled the net over the lip of the overhang, scraping Max and his bike roughly across the ice. The net fell open and the Arctirians grimaced.

"Oh! It's that rough boy!" one of them cried. "The one who destroyed half our city!

Why have you come here to bother us again?"

Max's temper flared. "I didn't destroy your city!" he said. "And I didn't come here to bother you either! I was swimming along, minding my own business, when your net scooped me out of the sea!"

The other Arctirian sighed. "And now I suppose we'll have to clean it," he said.

Max screwed up his watering eyes against the sun, and twitched his tingling nose. "Atchoo!" He let out a tremendous sneeze. Both Arctirians recoiled as if he had hit them.

"Oh, really!" one said. "I think you'd better get back in the water and swim away, taking your disgusting bodily functions with you!"

Max got to his feet. "I'd love to," he said, pushing his aquabike upright and wheeling it towards the edge of the cliff. "But first, tell me, have you seen Cora Blackheart recently?"

One of the Arctirians sniffed loudly,

and both stuck their narrow noses in the air. "There do seem to be rather a lot of unpleasant humans on the other side of the island, but we don't have anything to do with them. Hopefully they'll all go away soon and stop ruining our view of the sea."

"Okay, Max?" Rivet barked from below. The Arctirians peered over the cliff edge.

"Oh! That's truly hideous!" one said. The other gasped and pressed his hands to his chest, his blue eyes wide with rapture.

"Ah! But how lovely!" he breathed, gazing at Spike. "I remember this truly natural wonder. I could look at those graceful lines all day."

"Well, I'm afraid we're taking him with us!" Lia said crossly. Max leapt onto Sleekfin, and revved the engines. The Arctirians clapped their hands over their ears, while Max hit the accelerator and dived off the edge of the ice cliff.

As he plunged beneath the waves, Lia met him on Spike's back with Rivet at her side.

"So, there are humans on the other side of the island?" she said. "I guess that can only mean one thing."

Max nodded. "Cora and her evil crew. And I'm itching to find out what she's doing here in the freezing middle of nowhere!"

CHAPTER SEVEN

CORA'S PIRATE SHIP

As Max and Lia followed the shoreline of the island northwards, Max noticed that the whole coast seemed to be encased in ice. It formed swirling, pitted blue sculptures below the surface, and when Max looked up, he saw pale sunlight filtering through a translucent crust above.

They swam on, keeping close to the surface, until they rounded a high peninsula overshadowing the sea.

Max pulled up quickly and shut off his engines, signalling for Lia and Rivet to stop. Above them, near the shore, the clumps of sea ice were shattered like a dropped plate. And in the midst of the broken fragments floated a huge timber structure. *Cora's pirate ship!*

"Rivet?" Max said. "Can you scan the ship for any pirates?"

Rivet's eyes flashed red, and he ran them along the underbelly of the vessel. "No one there, Max!" Rivet barked.

Max grinned. "Perfect," he said. "Time for a bit of exploring. Maybe she's left the Arms of Addulis on board."

Max slid from Sleekfin's seat, letting the bike drift towards the seabed, while Lia strapped on her Amphibio mask.

"You'll have to stay here," she told Spike. "Keep watch and send me a warning if you catch sight of anything suspicious."

Max, Lia and Rivet kicked up towards the ice-free water alongside the bow of the ship. As they surfaced into the shadow of the curved hull, Max glanced hurriedly around to see if they'd been spotted. The sea and the icy shore beyond both seemed deserted. *Strange...* thought Max.

"Rivet, do you think you can get us up to the gunwale?" Max asked. Rivet lifted his nose, scanning the wooden hull.

"Easy, Max!" he said.

Max and Lia gripped tight to Rivet's collar, and the dogbot reached forwards and dug his claws into the wooden hull. It didn't take long for Rivet's strong, mechanical limbs to haul them up the side of the boat. Max grabbed the gunwale, then pulled himself over. Lia landed lightly beside him, and Rivet hit the deck with a thud.

Max glanced about, taking in the vessel's canvas sails, glass storm lanterns and polished wood and brass wheel. "Wow," he said. "This ship should be in a museum."

The wooden boards creaked and swayed underfoot as Max and Lia worked their way around the main deck, peering into every corner. They found barrels of pitch and piles of rope, but nowhere big enough to hide any of the Arms of Addulis.

"Let's head down to the hold," Max said. "That's where pirates normally store loot." He led Lia and Rivet down a narrow staircase onto a low, gloomy gun deck, where rows of hammocks swung. Beside each hammock stood a grimy-looking bucket. Max was suddenly very glad his nose was blocked.

Lia grimaced and held her hand in front of her mask. "If only this Amphibio mask had a filter!" she said. "Let's go before I pass out!"

"Smelly, Max!" Rivet barked, wagging his tail happily.

Max chuckled, then picked his way over the deck, careful not to get too close to any of the buckets. He followed another staircase down into an even darker,, dingier room. Worm-eaten barrels and bolts of cloth were stacked against a wall. The centre of the room was taken up by a huge wooden chest with brass straps and a hefty lock.

"This looks more like it!" Max said, crossing to the chest. He drew his hyperblade, expecting to have to smash the lock, but when he tried the lid, it opened easily. There was nothing inside but a bunch of scanners, blasters and other bits of tech.

"I thought that looked too good to be true," Lia said. "What about Cora's cabin?"

"It's worth a try," Max said. They headed back onto the main deck, then towards the raised poop deck at the bow. An ornate door carved with gilded scrollwork was set into the side. Max pushed the door, and it opened into a tidy room with a low bunk and a dressing table with a mirror. Rivet scrambled inside and started to sniff around.

"It doesn't look like Cora's your biggest fan," Lia said.

Covering half of one wall, dominating the small space, hung an enormous picture of Max. A gilded dagger was buried in Max's eye.

"You could be right there," Max said. He put his hand to the hilt of the dagger, and tugged it out. "Wha—!" Max leapt back as the wall before him spun, revealing a huge vidscreen.

Rivet growled. The screen blinked into life, and Cora's grinning face appeared. She was sitting in a modern control room, with the Helmet of Addulis perched on her head, and the Stone Breastplate covering her torso. In one hand, she held the Pearl Spear of Strength. The other rested on the Coral Sword, which lay across her lap. Max swallowed hard as a camera above the screen hummed and focussed on them.

Have we just walked into a trap?

"Welcome aboard," Cora said. She gave a contented sigh. "You two are so predictable. You've arrived right on cue. You just couldn't help yourselves, could you? Which is just as well, because if you hadn't fallen for my rather obvious decoy, I wouldn't be able to put my latest plan into action." Cora lifted a handheld control pad, and jabbed a button with one shiny black nail.

A deep throbbing started up, somewhere deep in the bowels of the vessel. The deck pitched, and the ship lurched forwards, slowly at first, but getting faster by the moment. Cora winked at Max.

"Have fun!" she said.

The vidscreen went blank. Max and Lia turned and sprinted back out onto the deck with Rivet at their heels. They found the ship crashing through ice, powering along the frozen shoreline.

A huge, man-made harbour slid into view as they rounded a peninsula. Small boats bobbed alongside a wooden jetty, and two metal scaffolds towered over the sea. Right in the centre of the harbour, glittering in the sun, an iceberg the size of a tanker rose up from the waves. Max's heart leapt into his mouth. The ship was heading right for it.

"Going to crash, Max!" Rivet barked.

Max took the stairs to the poop deck two at a time. He grabbed the ship's wheel and yanked. He pulled as hard as he could, throwing his weight into the movement, but the wheel didn't budge. Lia arrived at his side and added her strength to his. Rivet gripped a spoke with his teeth.

Nothing happened. It was stuck.

Max turned his attention back to the vast, blue-white iceberg ahead. 'Maybe we can jump onto the iceberg,' he shouted, charging to the front of the vessel, followed by the hurried footfalls of Lia and Rivet. Max skidded to a halt. His stomach clenched with fear. Inside

the translucent block of ice he could see a
long, dark, twisted shape. At one end was a set
of jagged teeth and a round black eye set into
a narrow head.

"Meet Jandor." Cora's voice blurted from

loudspeakers in the rigging above. "He's one of the Arctirians' prize exhibits. They trapped him in ice centuries ago, and I suspect that being cryogenically frozen hasn't improved his temper one bit. He's likely to be a bit of a handful. Unless, of course, you happen to have a magical Merryn Helmet that can control sea creatures like I do!"

Max stared at the frozen monster imprisoned in the ice, taking in its colossal size and the length of its triangular teeth. He'd never seen anything like it. Beside him, Lia was staring in awe, her knuckles white on the guardrail. The iceberg was gliding closer. They were only moments from impact.

"Get down!" Max cried, grabbing Lia by the arm. They threw themselves onto the deck, side by side. Rivet braced himself before them. Max tensed his muscles, preparing for the impact.

This is going to hurt!

STORY 2:

LIZARD FROM THE ICE

CHAPTER ONE

ANCIENT FURY UNLEASHED

CRASH! The ship careered into the iceberg with the sound of a thousand windows smashing.

The deck bucked, catapulting Max up over Rivet's metal back. He flew through the air, a hail of splintered timber and shattered ice pounding against his body.

Thud! His chest slammed against the guard rail, and he toppled back, gasping for breath. Lia landed in a tangle of limbs and silver hair beside him. Max tried to scramble up but his hands and knees skidded out from under him on the slippery wooden beams and his chin hit the deck. He looked up along the slanting planks to see the giant iceberg towering over him. A huge, jagged gash had been torn out of it, and the prow of the ship was leaning on the shelf of ice. The deck lurched sickeningly. Max clung to the wooden beams as the prow slid from its precarious perch on the iceberg and back into the sea.

SPLASH! Freezing spray splattered down on Max as the ship hit the waves, almost sinking beneath the surface. Max lay flat on the deck beside Lia as the boat heaved and rolled.

Once the rocking of the vessel had calmed, Max staggered up. What he saw ahead of him made him stop still. Lia grabbed his arm, her eyes wide with shock. The huge sea creature within the ice had begun to stir. The ice around it was cracking and tumbling into the sea. Massive chunks fell away to reveal a long, sinuous body, scaled like a crocodile, but with sharp fins like a shark's.

The Beast's muscular, paddle-like tail thrashed. Foaming waves and chunks of floating ice crashed against the ship, making it lurch and sway. Max only just managed to keep his balance, watching in fascinated horror as the vast, ancient animal before him twisted and flexed, forcing its body free. Finally, the ice that surrounded the monster's head shattered, revealing long, powerful jaws, a blunt snout and dark, sunken eyes. Jagged triangles of teeth with sharp serrated edges snapped at the air, and the dark eyes rolled with rage. Max gulped.

"Can you talk to it, Lia?" Max asked, his voice barely more than a croak.

Lia put her fingers to her temples, and

focussed on the creature's furious gaze. The ancient sea Beast shook its head, releasing a shower of icy shards, then lifted its jaws and let out a roar.

Max clamped his hands over his ears and braced his feet against the deck as a powerful blast of fishy air hit him, almost knocking him down. When the roaring finally stopped, Jandor fixed Max and Lia with its hollow-eyed stare, then dipped its massive head and slipped silently into the water, disappearing beneath the chunks of floating ice.

"It wouldn't listen," Lia said, weakly. "It's so angry. All I can sense from it is rage, and I don't blame it, being trapped all that time."

"Shouty fish gone, Max?" Rivet asked.

"I hope so, Riv," Max said, but as he spoke, the water beside the ship exploded in a shower of icy droplets and Jandor's massive head reared upwards. Max leapt back, his heart pounding. A scaled tower of muscular flesh loomed higher and higher over them.

"Abandon ship!" Max cried. He grabbed Lia's arm, and together they turned and raced towards the gunwale. Rivet was ahead of them as they dived into the sea.

As Max plunged through the freezing

waves, a thunderous crash echoed around him. Bubbles streamed in all directions, and a swirling current snatched at his limbs. Max used his arms and legs to right himself, and kicked back up to the surface. He found himself between the jagged halves of Cora's smashed ship. He looked around for the others but there was no sign of them. Above, he caught sight of barrels, trunks and hammocks teetering on the edge of the splintered deck. The two sections of ship began to sink. Max kicked his legs, swimming frantically out of the path of the vessel as the force of its motion sucked him back under the surface.

Below the waves, Max swam to a stop, and found broken planks and other debris swirling around him. In the chaos, he couldn't see Jandor, but the Beast had to be nearby. Lia and Rivet darted towards him through the churning water. They stopped, and Lia put her hands to her temples again, staring about her.

"Spike!" she said, "I can't find him!"

A pang of worry tugged at Max, but they couldn't look for Spike now. "Spike will be fine," Max said. "He'll have put as much distance between himself and that sea monster as possible. Which is what we need to do too." Max lifted his watch to his lips and summoned Sleekfin. A moment later, his aquabike darted through the churning debris. Max's heart swelled at the sight of his new invention. He leapt onto it.

"Get on!" he told Lia.

"But – Spike!"

"You can't help Spike from inside that creature's belly. Now get on!"

Lia hesitated. But then she gritted her teeth and swam onto the bike behind Max.

In his rear-view mirrors, Max could see Jandor's broad, blunt snout powering towards them.

"Cross fish coming, Max!" Rivet barked.

Max gunned the engines, hit the accelerator and shot forwards. "Keep close!" he called to Rivet. Jandor's long body snaked after them, carving effortlessly through the ocean with a powerful, muscular glide.

"Down, Riv!" Max cried, pushing on the handlebars of the aquabike. It lurched forwards, diving steeply as Max tried to lose the giant sea Beast, but the creature flicked its tail and followed, corkscrewing down through the water. Max steered sharp left and climbed, but Jandor was gaining. He engaged his rear-fin blasters, and took aim.

"No!" Lia cried, "It's not a robot, it's alive."

Max clenched his teeth in frustration. She was right. He couldn't kill it. But he wasn't ready to become fish food either. He slammed Sleekfin downwards, Rivet close behind, heading towards the seabed so fast his stomach flipped. Behind him, the creature twisted its body and swerved, slicing after the bike.

"Watch it, Rivet!" Max called. Jandor was snapping at the dogbot's heels. *I've got to help him.* Max pulled on the handlebars, zooming back across the Beast's path, luring its snapping jaws away from his pet. "Riv, hide!" he shouted.

Jandor writhed after the speeding aquabike, lunging for them madly.

"It's getting closer!" Lia shouted. Max's skin prickled with fear and Lia's arms clamped even tighter about his waist. He focussed on the seabed ahead. The shadowy forms of two boulders loomed out of the depths, and Max angled Sleekfin between them. He threw on the brakes and swerved sharply behind a rock. Lia thudded against him, and Rivet pulled up at his side as Jandor shot past.

BANG! Sleekfin's engines backfired at the sudden stop. Jandor's blunt snout whipped around. Its dark eyes flashed, and its giant wedge of a tail swept through the ocean. Max restarted his bike and gunned the engines, sending Sleekfin leaping forwards and away just as the tail slammed down.

CRUNCH! A cloud of choking dust exploded behind the bike, clogging Max's gills and stinging his eyes as he sped onwards. He glanced in his rear-viewers to see that Jandor had wheeled around and was zooming after them again.

It's so fast! Max thought. *Faster than Sleekfin. We have to get out of the water!* He swung his bike towards the shore. As the seabed sloped upwards, he could see the translucent crust of ice on the surface ahead. *If I can just get us up onto the ice…* Max glanced into his rear-viewer and every muscle in his body clenched with terror. Jandor's gaping mouth filled the view, and Max could smell the putrid fishy

stink of decay washing around him as the Beast prepared to swallow them whole.

CHAPTER TWO
JANDOR'S RAGE

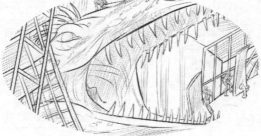

Max twisted the accelerator, his knuckles white. He steered sharply upwards, forcing every bit of speed from Sleekfin's engine. Beside him, Rivet was hurtling through the water, his propellers screaming as he tried to outrun the Beast. Lia clung to Max's waist so tight it was hard to breathe, but Max kept his eyes on the bright surface above, willing them to reach it before the jaws behind them snapped shut. *Nearly there…*

Sleekfin shot out of the water in a burst of

glittering spray. Icy wind swept past Max's face as his bike soared higher then started to fall. Max glanced down, and could just make out the ice shelf rushing up to meet them. *We made it!*

SMASH! Max jerked forwards, almost losing his seat as they hit the ice. He held on tight, trying to steer as the bike jack-knifed beneath him, crashing onto its side. Max's stomach somersaulted as he and Lia were thrown free. He skidded on the ice, the cold seeping through

his deepsuit, until finally he came to a stop. He blinked away his dizziness, shook the freezing water from his hair, then scrambled to his feet.

Lia was standing nearby, looking back towards the sea.

"Where is it?" Max said. He felt a faint vibration beneath his feet, getting stronger. Suddenly, Lia clutched his arm, and pointed downwards. Through the translucent ice beneath their feet, Max could make out a long, sinuous shape rising from the depths.

"Run!" he shouted. They turned and raced over the ice. Lia was struggling with her webbed toes, and Max could feel his feet skidding and slipping with each step. His heart thundered and his breath rasped. *Just don't slip*, he told himself.

SMASH! The sound of splintering ice filled the air and the slippery surface beneath

Max's feet shuddered. Max half stumbled, but caught himself and ran on. He glanced back to see Jandor's vast, scaled body hauling itself onto the ice. Its jaws clashed together in rage. Long cracks ran through the ice beneath its vast weight as Jandor lunged towards them, thrashing and rearing in rage.

Max and Lia raced towards solid ground, thin cracks spreading beneath their feet. Max could feel the ice sheet juddering. He could hear the echoing creak of it buckling beneath the Beast. He raced onwards. Each time he dared to glance back, he could see more cracks in the ice as the Beast slithered closer. Finally, just as Max thought his freezing lungs would burst, the splashing and splintering from behind stopped. Max slid to a halt. He looked back, panting, to see one of Jandor's dark eyes flash fiercely as it watched them. Then it turned and dived below the waves.

Lia stood beside him, with her hands to her temples and her eyes fixed on the ocean.

A dark shape was speeding towards the shore – two shapes, in fact. As Max watched, they resolved into the bulky metal form of Rivet, and Spike's graceful curves. Rivet broke the surface first. He shook his head fiercely, then clambered up onto the ice. Spike lifted his nose and clicked a greeting to Lia.

"Spike!" Lia said. "Thank goodness you're all right. But you need to hide until we've worked out what to do about Iandor."

Spike tipped his head back and let out another trill, then dipped below the waves.

Rivet shook his metal body all over, then turned to look out to sea.

"Grumpy fish!" he said.

Max grinned, slightly giddy from the adrenaline. "That's an understatement!" he said.

"You'd be grumpy too if someone had encased you in ice for centuries," Lia said.

Max nodded. "Not to mention being bossed about by Cora. But no matter how sorry we feel for Jandor, we still have to defeat it. Although, right now, I'm struggling to come up with ideas of how we can do that."

Lia shook her head. "You're looking at it all wrong," she said. "Jandor's not the problem. Cora's the one in control. If we can get Addulis's Helmet back, we won't need to worry about Jandor at all."

"True," Max said. "But I don't think Cora's just going to give it to us. She seems to be having far too much fun destroying things for that."

"So we'll have to take it," Lia said. "Along with the rest of Addulis's gear."

Max turned and gazed at Cora's bleak, industrial-looking base on the other side of the bay. A series of ugly metal huts looked out over the motorboats and hovercrafts moored alongside the narrow jetty. The two huge metal scaffolds Max had noticed before dominated the view. "You're right," Max said. "Let's head to her base and look for weak spots. Once we know what Cora is planning, we can stop her once and for all."

They turned inland and followed the coastline towards Cora's base. From the peninsula where they had been standing, the base had looked fairly close, but Max soon found that the view had been deceptive. He could see the tips of Cora's giant scaffolds on the horizon, but no matter how quickly they walked through the snow, they didn't seem to get any closer. Lia's webbed feet let her step lightly on the crust of the snow without breaking through, and Rivet's mechanical legs ploughed through the drifts effortlessly. Max watched them enviously as he waded through, panting and sweating while shivering at the same time. His knees and back ached as he pushed onwards, and the light reflecting from the white surface pierced his eyes.

"Okay, Max?" Rivet suddenly barked, startling Max so that he stumbled. Lia caught his arm, preventing him from falling face-first into the snow. Rivet had stopped and was looking back at Max, his head on one side. "Need medicine, Max?" Rivet asked.

Of course! With a rush of relief, Max realised he wasn't just being weak. He was sick! He nodded gratefully, and took a strand of sourweed from Rivet's hatch. This time, as he chewed the tough weed between his teeth, it didn't taste nearly so bad, and he felt his aches and pains recede and his strength begin to return.

After that, they made better progress. It wasn't long before they crested a rise in the snow, to find Cora's base spread out before them. The sound of rough voices raised in a sea shanty reached them on the breeze. Max and Lia ducked back behind the snowdrift. They shimmied forwards on their elbows and knees, and peered over the snowy rise towards the harbour.

Lia gasped. "The poor creature!" she cried.

Max shook his head, pity welling inside him. "That's just not right!" he said.

Jandor was suspended high above the sea in a pair of slings gripped by metal dock-clamps. The huge scaffolds Cora had built stood on either side of the sea Beast. Max could see pirates clambering up and down, fixing metal plates and what looked like blasters and knives to Jandor's scaly skin. The mighty Beast lay perfectly still, but its deep-

set eyes were darting fearfully backwards and forwards, watching the pirates work. On the jetty stood Cora, wearing the Helmet of Addulis. Max could hear her sharp voice carrying on the wind as she shouted orders to her crew.

"Hurry up, you worthless maggots!" she shrieked. "We don't have all day!"

Lia turned to Max with a puzzled expression. "Cora's controlling Jandor with the Helmet to stop it fighting back. But why? What is she doing to it?"

Max let out a shaky breath, trying to hold back the tide of fear and anger building inside him. "She's making her own Robobeast, that's what," Max said. "One she can control herself, but not with technology. She's going to control it with her own twisted mind."

CHAPTER THREE

DESPERATE PLANS

Max, Lia and Rivet scrambled down the side of the snowdrift and crept towards Cora's base. They dodged between ice-covered rocks and mounds of snow, keeping their bodies low to the ground. When they were a stone's throw away from Cora's giant scaffolds, they crouched behind a rock, and peered out at the base. Cora was gazing up at the metal-clad form of Jandor suspended in the giant dock clamps. She was dressed in a grey deepsuit, her dark hair hanging in matted waves from under her magical helmet. In one hand, she held the Pearl Spear, and in the other, a jewelled chalice.

"More grog, you stinking sea slugs!" Cora cried, waving her cup. A scrawny young pirate with boils on his jaw rushed to her side

and filled her cup. Cora drained it in one go, then shoved her empty cup towards him. The lanky pirate filled the cup again from his flask.

"Right!" Cora said, after taking another gulp. "Get that control panel fixed on beside the saddle and I'll be just about ready to ride!"

A pair of pirates on the scaffold were holding a metal plate covered in dials and buttons between them. They pressed it against the metalwork covering Jandor's body and started to attach it, screwdrivers whining.

Cora's going to ride the Beast!

"Come on, you pox-ridden puke rags!" Cora shrieked. "The sooner we finish this re-fit, the sooner we can head over to the Chaos Quadrant and take control. We'll raise a pirate army the likes of which have never been seen before. The Aquorans won't know what's hit them! And when those lily-livered landlubbers surrender – which they'll do sharpish if they want to keep all their limbs – we'll keelhaul the lot of them!" Cora raised her hands, drawing a rowdy cheer from her crew. "We'll sell Mr and Mrs Max North into slavery," she went on. "I reckon they'll look good scouring timbers, don't you?" The pirates let out another chorus of whistles and cheers, then scurried around faster than ever, fixing the last touches to Jandor's hide.

Max fumed as he watched Cora swigging back grog and barking orders. *She's lost it this time,* he thought. *But with the Arms of Addulis, she might actually be able to put her crazy plan into action.*

"We have to stop her!" he muttered to Lia. "We must recover the Arms of Addulis and set that poor sea Beast free."

Lia didn't reply. Max turned and his stomach sank. She was gone.

He spotted a line of footprints in the snowy

ground and followed them with his eyes. *Oh no!* Lia was hunched at the base of one of the dock clamps, fiddling with a bank of controls.

She's going to set Jandor free, Max realised. But as Lia poked at buttons and turned dials, he could see she didn't have a clue. *I have to help her.* Except that Lia was only a few paces from Cora and there were pirates everywhere.

Lia put her fingers to her temples and gazed at Jandor, trying to communicate with her Aqua Powers. The creature's head snapped around. It opened its giant mouth and let out a long, sad wail.

All the pirates turned and stared at Lia. She dropped her hands and stood tall, staring back with furious eyes.

Well, there goes our element of surprise! Max thought. "Wait here!" he told Rivet, then he leapt to his feet and sped over the icy ground towards Lia.

"How dare you!" Lia shouted. "How dare you trap an innocent creature?" The pirates stared at her in confusion, but then Cora let out a cackle.

"Put a stop to her meddling, would you?" she said, waving a hand at the pirate nearest Lia. The pirate lifted his pistol, narrowed his eyes and aimed. Max ran shoulder-first towards him, his feet pounding over the slippery ground. Lia jumped out of the line of the shot just as Max thudded into the pirate's side. The pistol flew through the air, firing as it went, and the pirate careered over the edge of the ice sheet into the freezing water below.

Another pirate rounded on Max with a snarl, and drew his hyperblade cutlass. The man was missing several teeth, and Max could smell the rotten stink of his breath along with fumes of grog coming off his pasty skin. Max swung his own hyperblade.

Clang! The pirate's blade met his. Max swung again, harder this time, driving the pirate back with swipe after swipe. As Max jabbed and parried, he could see Lia from the corner of his eye, stabbing her spear towards a stocky pirate woman.

A second man leapt to the side of the

toothless pirate facing Max. As Max stepped back to get his breath, both pirates grinned and raised their cutlasses. Max lunged forwards, his blade flashing through the air, but then he felt something hard smash into the back of his head. His vision blurred and his body crumpled. The icy ground slammed up to meet him, and his hyperblade flew from his hand. Max heard a thud, and the sound of Lia crying out nearby. He blinked to clear his vision and saw her lying beside him in the snow. A ring of hairy, grubby pirates surrounded them.

"Wait, lads!" Cora barked. "Don't kill them yet." The pirates backed away and Cora strutted forwards to stand by Max's feet. Max's eyes were still swimming in and out of focus, but he could see the pirate captain's evil grin as she set her cup of grog down on the scaffold beside her. Max lay on his back, blinking up at Cora, his head throbbing and his body wracked with violent shivers.

How are we going to get out of this? he wondered. *Even if I had my full strength, we could never fight all these pirates, and with my gill pox, we don't stand a chance.* Max thought of the sourweed in Rivet's pouch. He could really do with some now.

Then, looking up at Cora's evil, grinning face, something clicked into place in his brain. *I need to level the playing field...* he thought.

"Stall her!" Max hissed to Lia. Lia gave the merest hint of a nod, then sat bolt upright, and started to shout.

"Let Jandor go!" she cried, punching the air with her fist. "How can you be so cruel? So barbaric?!" Cora burst out laughing, and her pirate crew joined in. Max took the chance Lia had given him. He twitched his nose, blinked as if he was going to sneeze, then lifted his communicator watch to his lips, while pretending to rub his nose. "Rivet!" Max hissed. "Put the sourweed in Cora's grog." Then he quickly lowered his hand.

Cora finally stopped laughing, and spat at the ground. "Thank you for your advice, little princess," she said, shoving Lia back onto the snow with sole of her robotic foot. "But sadly I don't share your pathetic Merryn obsession with brainless sea creatures. No. I've got plans for that oversized sea snake. Plans that start with killing you two."

Cora clicked her fingers, and the pirates that surrounded Max and Lia stepped forwards. Max flinched as rough hands grabbed his arms. The pirates hauled him to his feet, and Max glanced towards the scaffolding beside Cora. He had to stifle a smile. Rivet was resting his front paws on the wooden board that held Cora's cup, and as Max watched, the

dogbot let something fall from his jaws into the grog. Sourweed. Lots of sourweed. A fizz of bubbles rose up from the cup and Rivet vanished behind a dock clamp.

"Get those puny children up onto the scaffold!" Cora screeched. "It's time for our uninvited guests to walk the plank!"

CHAPTER FOUR

WALKING THE PLANK

Max stood on a narrow wooden plank at the top of the towering scaffolding, his boots pressed tightly together and the point of a cutlass pricking at his back. Lia was just ahead of him, swaying slightly, her hair fluttering in the bitter wind. Max glanced down, and swallowed. Far below, chunks of ice were clashing together, rising and falling on foaming, turquoise waves.

A sharp dorsal fin cut the surface, then

disappeared. *Spike!* The sight of Lia's swordfish gave Max a glimmer of hope. He quickly pressed a button on his watch. "Sleekfin, come!" he said, summoning his bike from the ice shelf where he'd left it.

"It's a long drop!" Cora called up to them. "But please try to survive. I want to see what my new pet fish can do."

Glancing down and to his right, Max could see Cora standing beside the vast, still form of Jandor. The giant Beast had been lowered until its armoured belly hung just above the waves. Cora downed the rest of her grog and tossed the cup over her shoulder, then leapt lightly onto Jandor's broad back. She settled herself in her leather saddle, and slotted Addulis's Sword and Spear into holsters on the harness. A breathing mask dangled around her neck, and she pulled it up over her face, before leaning forward to reach the

control panel by her hand. Each button she touched set one of Jandor's new guns moving with a clank and a hum.

"All set!" Cora called at last to a greasy-looking brute of a pirate holding a winch on the dock. "Time for a test run."

The pirate's massive arm muscles bulged, and the winch started to turn. Vast chains clanked and Cora gave a whoop as she and

Jandor were lowered into the sea.

As Jandor's belly touched the water, Cora looked back up at Max. Her dark eyes were the only part of her face visible between her helmet and mask, but Max could tell she was grinning. "I think the Beast is hungry!" she called up.

A sharp shove between the shoulder blades sent Max cannoning forwards into Lia. Lia gasped, her hands grabbing at the air as she toppled off the plank. Max's foot plunged into nothingness and he tumbled after her, the sea rushing up to meet them.

SPLASH! Brain-numbing cold filled Max's senses. He couldn't breathe or see. He couldn't even tell which way was up. His teeth were clamped together and all his muscles had locked. He forced himself to relax, to draw water in through his gills, and blinked, looking for Lia. He spotted her nearby, struggling to pull off her Amphibio mask as Spike dived beneath her and scooped her onto his back. Lia finally tugged the mask away, and Max struck out through the water towards her, his freezing arms and legs somehow pushing him forwards. But before he could reach Lia, he saw a huge, dark slab of scaled muscle sweep towards her. Jandor's massive tail.

"Lia, move!" Max cried.

Spike was already swimming, his silvery sword slicing away from the giant sea Beast, but Max could see it was too late. Jandor's tail slammed into Spike's side and sent him spinning away. Lia flew from Spike's back into the shadowy water beneath the sea-ice.

Jandor's thick, muscled body swished past Max as the Beast turned to face him. Cora was craning forwards in her seat, her eyes lit up with excitement. Max's skin tightened with horror as two massive blasters either side of

Jandor's head swivelled towards him. His hand reached instinctively for his missing hyperblade as his chest tightened with fear.

Suddenly a black shape trailing bubbles plunged into the water before Max. As the bubbles cleared, Max saw Rivet powering towards the Robobeast.

"Rivet to the rescue!" the dogbot barked, his motors throbbing as he charged.

"Rivet! Get back!" Max cried, just as a tremendous boom shattered the calm under the waves.

A white energy bolt sliced through the water from one of Jandor's cannons and smashed into Rivet's metal body. *No!* Max's heart leapt as his dogbot yelped and tumbled away into the freezing depths. But he couldn't help Rivet now. He had a much bigger problem to face. Cora and her giant Robobeast.

Jandor's massive tail flicked, and its snake-like body hurtled forwards. The Beast's long jaws snapped open revealing yellow, saw-like teeth.

CHAPTER FIVE

THE MOMENT BEFORE DEATH

Time seemed to slow for Max as the giant Robobeast carved towards him. He found he could see every detail of the creature's broad, scaled face. Its sunken green eyes were so dark they were almost black, and the pupils were narrow slits. Inside the Beast's mouth, rows of triangular teeth curved inwards. They looked sharp enough to shear through bone.

From Jandor's back, Cora was shouting victorious chants. Max could hardly hear them. His mind was blank, except for one heart-stopping thought. *I'm going to die.*

A low throbbing sound cut through his strange, altered senses – a sound which filled him with hope. Max turned to see Sleekfin revving towards him. Relief flooded through his body. "See you later, Cora!" he shouted, kicking up onto his bike and slamming it around. He raced away from the Robobeast.

"You can run but you can't escape me!"

Cora's voice shrieked. Max heard a crackling sound, and two silver energy beams shot past his face, smashing craters in the seabed ahead. Max glanced in his rear-viewers, and found the tip of Jandor's nose almost touching the back of his bike. He couldn't see any sign of Lia.

Cora's right! Max realised. *I can't escape. I need to fight.* He tapped a command into Sleekfin's control panel, programming his new bike to release its fuel. In his rear-viewers, he saw an oily green cloud spew out into the water, obscuring his view of the Beast. *If I can't see them, maybe they can't see me...* Max tipped backwards off his bike, then kicked his legs, and swam downwards as fast as he could. Once he reached the dark water near the seabed, he dived inside a clump of billowing weed, and peered out. The silver form of his bike roared past overhead, stuttering and losing height, still trailing a slick of green fuel.

BOOM! It ploughed straight into the seabed, and exploded in a ball of yellow flames. They flared brightly for a moment, before extinguishing to a dull orange glow. A moment later, Jandor's vast, sinuous form shot out of the green fuel cloud, and came to an abrupt halt over the steaming wreck.

From his hiding place amongst the seaweed fronds, Max could see Cora, peering down from her seat on Jandor's back. She frowned as she scanned the seabed for signs of his corpse.

I'm not going to get a better chance than this! Max thought. He waited until Cora was glancing the other way, then darted up from his hiding place towards Jandor's armoured belly. Max hugged close to the shining metal attached to Jandor's body, then swam up and onto the creature's back. He crept over the armour plates towards Cora, looking for

a point of attack. *If I can just get Addulis's Helmet off her, Jandor will be free...* But as Max reached his hand towards Cora's head, she spun in her seat, and swiped his arm away.

"Thought you'd creep up on me, did you?" she sneered. "Well, think again!" Cora's hand flicked to the control panel at her side, and Jandor shot forwards. Max just managed to grab the tip of the Robobeast's tail as it swept past beneath him.

"Whoa!" His arms were jerked painfully as he flew through the ocean, tugged by the speeding reptile. Water whooshed past him, threatening to pull him free. He gritted his teeth and lifted a hand, using all his strength to push it through the current flowing around him. He reached as far as he could and clamped his fingers around the edge of a scale on Jandor's back. Then he began to climb hand over hand, pulling himself forwards. Water filled his eyes and rushed past his gills so fast he could hardly catch his breath, but he climbed on until he was almost in reach of Cora's seat.

"Oh, give up, will you?" Cora shouted, grabbing her Spear in one hand, and tapping a button on her controls. Jandor slammed suddenly to a stop and Max's fingers were torn from their grip. He shot off into the ocean, his arms and legs flailing as he tried to stop himself. Cora leapt up and wheeled around, twirling her Spear towards him. Jandor floated still and docile in the water beneath her, controlled by Addulis's Helmet.

"Come on!" Cora cried. "If you want a fight, I'm ready." She held Addulis's Spear in one hand, and his Sword in the other.

Max's mouth went as dry as sand. *Fight with what?* Max thought. *My teeth? This is hopeless!* Then he caught a flicker of movement from the corner of his eye. *Is that...?* He snatched a quick glance into the water behind Cora, and saw something that filled him with courage and hope. Spike was darting towards Jandor, with Lia on his back. *I just have to distract Cora for long enough for them to reach me...* Max thought.

He swam down to stand on Jandor's broad back, and met Cora's furious stare.

"Even if you kill me," Max said, "there's no way you'll take Aquora. Not while my father's in charge. You've failed before, and you'll fail again. It's what pirates like you do best." He could see Spike clearly now, and Lia raising her spear.

Cora shrugged. "I'll take my chances," she said. "But first I'm going to enjoy finishing you off!" Cora lunged, jabbing for Max with the Pearl Spear. At the same moment, Lia drew back her arm and let her own spear fly. Max leapt aside, dodging Cora's strike, but Cora darted after him. Lia's spear flew past, missing the pirate by a hand's breadth and hitting Jandor's armour with a clang. Max snatched the spear up as it bounced off Jandor's back, and jabbed for Cora as she lunged again. Their spears met with a crash that threw Max backwards. He righted himself in the water, and turned his spear on

Cora as she swiped for him with her Sword.
Max managed to block the blow with the
shaft of his spear, but it left his arms ringing
with pain.

Max leapt back, dodging Cora's flickering
blade. His breath rasped through his gills,
and he was starting to feel dizzy and sick
again from the pox. Cora lifted her Sword and
Spear and smiled. Behind her, Max could see
Spike and Lia coming in for another strike.

Spike's long sword was aimed at Cora's back, but as he got close, Jandor's razor teeth snapped towards him, and he darted back out of reach.

Cora stalked towards Max over Jandor's back, her Sword and Spear raised. Max looked at the thick armour plate covering her chest and the mystical weapons in her hands, and his gut clenched with fear.

I don't have a hope.

The evil pirate's black eyes glinted above her breathing mask, and she darted forward with unnatural speed. Max kicked upwards off Jandor's back, and thrust his spear downwards. Cora's Sword sliced upwards in an arc. The blade met the shaft of Max's spear, smashing it from his grasp. Cora leapt, her booted foot flying up almost too fast for Max to see. It thudded into his chest, driving him backwards through the water.

Max gasped for breath as he tumbled down onto Jandor's back. Cora leapt over him, her eyes narrowed and her black hair snaking around her in the current.

"Enough of these games!" she snapped. Then she lifted the Pearl Spear of Strength, aiming its glinting point at Max's heart.

CHAPTER SIX

BATTLE ON THE SEABED

Max's whole body thrummed to the beat of his pulse. His muscles were tense, ready to fight or run, but he had nowhere to go, and nothing to fight with. His stomach clenched with fear. *This has to be it*, he thought. *The end...* Max looked up into Cora's fierce black eyes, trying to prepare himself for the final, fatal blow. Then he saw her blink. Her whole body swayed.

The sourweed! Triumph swelled in Max's

chest. Cora swayed again, then staggered forwards. Max rolled aside, and watched as Cora plunged the tip of the Pearl Spear straight through the metal armour covering Jandor's back. The Beast thrashed, and Cora lost her grip on the Spear and tumbled onto Jandor's back.

Max dived forward, reaching desperately for her Helmet, but Cora's eyes snapped into focus. She lifted her knee and drove it hard into Max's gut. He fell back, curling into a ball. Bile rose in his throat, and he sucked water through his gills to fight the sickness. He looked up to see Cora standing over him, tugging a blaster pistol from her belt, and taking aim. Terror seared through Max's veins, but then he noticed Cora frowning hard as she tried to focus through the fog of the sourweed. She pulled the trigger, and her blaster shot zoomed off into the ocean, well wide of its mark.

"What is happening to me?" Cora muttered, frowning groggily at her shaking hand. Max pulled himself up to stand before her.

"I spiked your grog with sourweed," Max said. "A lot of it. I expect you'll pass out soon."

"Not before I kill you!" Cora growled.

She pulled the trigger, and Max ducked, lunging for Cora's legs. They crashed together onto Jandor's back, and Max leapt on top of Cora, pinning her sword arm down and grabbing again for her Helmet. This time he managed to hook his fingers under the edge of the shell near her chin, and tugged it free.

Yes!

Cora screamed in rage, bubbles streaming from her breathing mask, but her cry stopped suddenly as Jandor's vast body rolled out from beneath her. Max grabbed the shaft of the Pearl Spear as Jandor dipped away. The weapon held for a moment, stuck in the giant Beast's back. Water buffeted against Max and his arm muscles screamed as he gripped the Spear tightly, but then the Beast thrashed, and the Spear came free. Max tumbled backwards through the water, holding the Pearl Spear, as Jandor flicked his colossal tail and powered away.

Cora was drifting slowly towards the ocean floor, rubbing her eyes. Max dived after her. As he kicked towards the seabed, he gripped the Pearl Spear of Addulis in both hands, feeling the awesome strength of the creatures of the deep powering through his veins.

He pulled back the Spear and sent it smashing into Cora's back. There was a mighty boom as the magical weapon hit Cora's Breastplate, and Cora was dashed against the rocky ocean floor. She shook herself and leapt to her feet, scowling, then lunged at Max, swinging the Sword of Speed.

Max darted back and Cora's clumsy strike sliced harmlessly through the water. She lurched forwards, carried by the weight of her stroke, and Max sent his Spear in a low arc, swiping her legs from under her. Cora let out a howl of fury and leapt up, but Max jabbed her in the Breastplate with his Spear,

shoving her down again.

Suddenly he felt the seabed judder beneath his feet, and a moment later deep booms echoed towards him on the current. He glanced towards the sound to see Jandor striking his vast body against the rocky ocean floor, smashing metal plates and weapons off his hide into the water.

He's freeing himself from Cora's tech!

Quickly Max sent the butt of his Spear lashing towards Cora's fingers where she clasped the hilt of the Sword.

"Aargh!" The Sword fell from Cora's hand.

She bent to pick it up, but Max swung his Spear once more, sending her rolling across the seabed. Max leapt over her and lifted his Spear, aiming its sharp, pearl-tipped point at the exposed skin of her neck.

Cora glared at him, and Max had never seen such venomous hate. "You won't kill

me!" Cora said. "You haven't got the guts!"

"Guts have got nothing to do with it!" Max said. He jabbed the Spear down towards the clasp at Cora's shoulder that fastened her Breastplate. The clasp sprang open, and the Breastplate fell from her chest. "You need to face Aquoran justice," Max said. "And you can't do that if you're dead."

Suddenly Cora's eyes shot wide open, and she let out a shriek. Max turned to follow her terrified gaze. Jandor was speeding towards them. The Beast's scales were smooth and sleek, and it moved with astonishing grace now the armour plates that had weighed it down were gone. It thrust forwards through

the water, its huge eyes filled with dark rage and its mighty jaws parted in what looked horribly like a grin.

CHAPTER SEVEN
A NEW EXHIBIT

Max's blood froze in his veins. There was no way he could stop Jandor without hurting the Beast. But if he didn't, he was dead.

Cora let out a terrified whimper as Jandor surged closer. Max's whole body was trembling, and he couldn't take his eyes off the creature's dark-eyed stare. Then, as Jandor's huge head filled Max's view and his heart thundered as if it might burst, the giant Beast stopped dead, a sub's length away.

Jandor's jagged teeth snapped shut, and the look of fury in its sunken eyes softened to puzzled interest.

Max watched the Beast for a long moment, unsure whether to stay or turn and swim for his life. Then he noticed a flicker of movement above the Beast's giant head. Lia shot out from behind it, riding Spike and wearing the Helmet of Addulis. In one hand she clasped her spear, in the other Max's hyperblade.

"I thought you could do with some help," Lia said, grinning smugly as Max gaped at her. Relief washed over him in dizzying waves. He took back his weapon, and sheathed it.

Jandor slowly lifted its long snout towards Lia, and she ran her webbed fingers over the Beast's domed head. The creature's huge eyes narrowed with pleasure, and Lia grinned.

"Don't let him eat me!" Cora whimpered

from behind Max.

Lia wrinkled her nose. "He's got better taste than that!" she said. "But I've told him there are some nasty pirates up near the surface who need to be taught a lesson." She lifted her hand from Jandor's massive head, and Spike carried her a short distance away.

"Be free, friend!" Lia told the Beast. Jandor

turned his head, flicked his tail, and shot off towards the bay.

Max watched him go, then pulled a long, deep draught of water over his gills, forcing his trembling body to relax. "Nice timing!" Max managed shakily. Lia grinned, and ran her eyes over the ocean floor. Max saw her taking in the fallen Sword and Breastplate of Addulis, the barely conscious form of Cora, and Rivet, who Max saw was clambering slowly to his feet nearby. *Thank goodness he's okay!* Max thought.

"It looks like you've had quite a battle!" Lia said, swimming over to the Sword and Breastplate and scooping them up, then fastening her own spear to her back.

A tremendous crash echoed through the water from the direction of Cora's base, and Max winced. "It sounds like it's not over yet," he said. "Let's head up to the surface and see what's going on." He turned to Rivet, who was scanning the debris, looking dazed. "Okay, Riv?" Max asked.

Rivet paddled over to Max, then nosed at Cora's slumped body. "Bad lady sick, Max?" Rivet asked.

"Just sleeping, Riv," Max said. "Do you think you can carry her to the surface?"

"Yes, Max!" Rivet barked.

Max took a coil of cord from Rivet's back compartment, and tied Cora's wrists together. Her eyelids fluttered as he lifted her onto Rivet's back, and she murmured something before slumping forwards again. Max tied her to his dogbot, then nodded to Lia.

"All set," he said. "Let's go."

Max, Lia, Rivet and Spike powered to the surface, Rivet carrying the sleeping Cora with him. When Max broke through the waves into daylight, he glanced towards Cora's base and couldn't help grinning. It was in total chaos. Jandor had forged a path through the ice, right into the bay, and was splintering the wooden dock with swipes of his massive tail. His huge body soared out of the water and his vast jaws snapped shut on

one of Cora's scaffolds, tearing a mouthful of metal away.

Pirates were racing about like ants, and Max could hear their panicked screams as Jandor continued to snap and thrash, destroying everything in his path. Some of the pirates leapt into the freezing ocean, while others

tried to flee inland, but Jandor lurched towards them, smashing the ice beneath their feet and sending them screaming into the waves. Some managed to scramble into motorboats, and fired the thrusters, shooting away from the shore.

"Jandor's not very happy about being experimented on," Lia said.

Max watched in fascinated awe as Jandor's lithe body snaked through the water after the retreating boats, leaving a foaming trail in its wake.

"He's looking forward to pirate-hunting," Lia said, grinning. "He hasn't had a fresh meal in centuries."

There was a soft whirr of engines from behind, and Max turned to see an elegant blue boat gliding towards them. His heart sank. *Just what we need.* The two Arctirians that had caught him in their net were standing at the prow, surveying the wreckage of Cora's bay. They cut the engines of their vessel and pulled up beside Max, frowning.

"What carnage is this?" one of the glowing creatures asked. "This view will take years to restore. And why has Jandor been released? He was our prize exhibit. Irreplaceable. A

historical artefact we've had on display since the founding days of Arctiria."

Max gestured to Cora, still slumped over Rivet's back, her head lolling and her mouth hanging slackly open. "Blame the pirate," Max said. "It was her doing." Then Max had an idea. "Maybe you could take her instead?" he said. "You could call the exhibit, er… *The Ugliness of Evil*?"

The Arctirians eyed Cora's bedraggled form, and wrinkled their narrow noses. "It's certainly unusually hideous," one said. "Look at its greasy hair!"

"True," said the other. "But its metal leg is rather novel. We don't have anything like that. Maybe it would make an interesting piece for a tank in the servants' quarters?"

The other sighed. "I suppose so," he said. "They could keep it as a sort of pet. Does it eat worms?"

Max nodded, untying Cora from Rivet's back. "Worms and insects," he said. "It's not really very fussy."

The Arctirians lifted Cora's body into their boat, and nodded a haughty goodbye to Max and Lia. As they powered away, Lia turned to Max, frowning anxiously.

"The Arctirians seem a little…trusting," she said. "Aren't you worried that Cora will escape?"

Max grinned. "One day, I expect she will," he said. "But when she does, we'll be ready." Max twirled the Pearl Spear in his hand, enjoying the surging strength it gave him. "Now, I suppose we'd better get the Arms of Addulis back to Sumara…"

Lia's hand brushed the Coral Helmet she still wore on her head, and she darted forwards with a few lightning-quick stabs of the Sword of Speed. "I don't know, I could get used to these."

"Not sure your father would be too happy if we kept them," said Max, grinning. "Come on, let's go. I just wish I hadn't lost Sleekfin. The journey's going to take ages without a bike."

"Um. It's not exactly lost," Lia said, pointing to the seabed below. "But it doesn't look quite the same."

The blackened skeleton of Max's bike lay beneath the clear turquoise water. Max ducked below the surface, and swam down to inspect it. The fabric seat had burned away, and the rubber seals had melted, but the metal bodywork seemed mostly undamaged. Max kicked back up to the surface.

"I reckon I can fix it," he said. "I'll get Rivet to tow it back with us."

Lia shrugged. "It still won't be nearly as good as a real swordfish," she said, stroking Spike's back.

Once Max had tied Sleekfin to Rivet, they set off southwards. Max found he was actually enjoying the swim, and realised he hadn't sneezed in ages.

"Hey!" he said. "I think my gill pox is almost gone! Which just goes to show, Tarla

doesn't know everything. She wanted me to rest, but it was a Sea Quest that cured my bug."

Lia turned back to him and rolled her eyes. "I told you it wasn't serious," she said.

"Well, I'm just glad I'm better. It means I can get stuck into fixing my bike when we get back. And you and your dad can work out a safer place to store the Arms of Addulis. They're too powerful to fall into the wrong hands again."

Lia shot Max an irritated look, but then she shrugged her shoulders and smiled. "It doesn't matter," she said. "The bad guys don't stand a chance. Whatever happens, we'll be ready to stop them!"

Don't miss the next Sea Quest book,
in which Max faces

VELOTH
THE VAMPIRE SQUID

Read on for a sneak preview!

CHAPTER ONE

BLACKOUT!

Max twisted the wheel of his new sailsub as it passed the marker buoy, which glowed pink in the Aquoran evening. The vessel tipped sharply and Max had to lean backwards out over the edge to keep it balanced. His head missed the buoy by mere inches but he needed to take some risks if he was going to catch up with Lia.

He looked up to see his friend briefly break the surface of the water before diving back under, hardly causing a ripple. She was well ahead of him and increasing the gap. Max was starting to regret challenging her to a race, especially before he'd had a chance to get used to the sailsub's controls. But he'd been so excited about trying out the clever new design that he couldn't wait. The vessel's hull was the size of a large Aquoran car and was shaped like a slightly flattened egg when viewed from the side. It had a small cockpit, fins for control and a retractable keel which was used when the sailsub was on the surface.

A sudden, fierce gust of wind gave Max some hope and he pulled in the mainsail to take advantage of it. The sailsub leapt ahead as if it had been stung and Max saw that he was gaining on Lia. There was still just enough sunlight left for him to see her sleek shape racing under the surface, her webbed feet kicking her along.

I'm catching up with her!

But then Lia turned over on to her back, grinning. Max was confused, until the Merryn girl gave him a wave, kicking hard and shooting ahead at what seemed like double speed. The next moment the wind changed and the sailsub slowed to a crawl.

"Try the spinnaker, Max," a voice crackled in his earpiece. It was Niobe, Max's mother. He could just make her out, watching from the dock, silhouetted against the blazing harbour lights. "The wind should be directly behind you now."

Max didn't need telling twice. He flipped a switch on the console and felt the clunk and grind of the shimmering sail unfurling at the very front of the sailsub. It was made from a lightweight metal fabric and caught the breeze instantly. The sail strained forward, hauling the vessel along behind.

Lia didn't seem bothered. She was toying with him now, flitting back and forth around the vessel. Max gritted his teeth in frustration. "So that's the spinnaker, is it?" Lia said via Max's headset. "Very pretty. But you can't catch me, however many sails you use." She streaked ahead past the next glowing buoy. Lia was just too fast, and getting faster.

Wind power is great, Max thought, but it can't beat a big turbo engine. He looked down to a large red button on the control panel. He shrugged and slammed his fist down on it. It's cheating, but only a little!

A plexiglass canopy slid out and enclosed the cockpit as the keel retracted and the two sails folded back into the craft's body, locking themselves away in neat compartments. Max felt a thrill at the rumble of the turbo engines firing up and thrusting the sailsub forwards and then down, under the surface. Bubbles of trapped air raced across the canopy. It took Max's eyes a moment to adjust to the undersea conditions. Ever since Lia had given him the Merryn Touch he'd had excellent vision under the sea, and now up ahead he could see her form, racing away from him.

Max pushed the thruster control to full power and the sailsub shot after her, pressing him back into the cushioned seat. It took just a few seconds to catch up with the Merryn princess. As Max zoomed beneath her, overtaking, he looked up through the transparent canopy and waved. Lia looked furious. That's turbo power!

COLLECT THEM ALL!

SERIES 7:

THE LOST STARSHIP

978 1 40834 064 6

978 1 40834 066 0

978 1 40833 480 5

978 1 40834 070 7

www.seaquestbooks.co.uk

DISCOVER THE FIRST SERIES
OF SEA QUEST:

978 1 40831 848 5

978 1 40831 849 2

978 1 40831 850 8

978 1 40831 851 5

SPECIAL BUMPER BOOK ✷

DON'T MISS THE NEXT SPECIAL BUMPER BOOK:

REPTA
THE SPIKED BRUTE!

978 1 40834 072 1

www.seaquestbooks.co.uk

WIN AN EXCLUSIVE GOODY BAG

In every Sea Quest book the Sea Quest logo is
hidden in one of the pictures. Find the logo in this book,
make a note of which page it appears on and
go online to enter the competition at

www.seaquestbooks.co.uk

Each month we will put all of the correct entries into a draw
and select one winner to receive a special Sea Quest goody bag.

You can also send your entry on a postcard to:

Sea Quest Competition,
Orchard Books, Carmelite House
50 Victoria Embankment
London EC4Y 0DZ

Don't forget to include your name and address!

GOOD LUCK

Closing Date: 29th February 2016

Competition open to UK and Republic of Ireland residents. No purchase required.
For full terms and conditions please see www.seaquestbooks.co.uk

DARE YOU DIVE IN?

Deep in the water lurks a new breed of Beast.

If you want the latest news and exclusive Sea Quest goodies, join our Sea Quest Club!

Visit www.seaquestbooks.co.uk/club and sign up today!

IF YOU LIKE SEA QUEST, YOU'LL LOVE BEAST QUEST!

Series 1: COLLECT THEM ALL!

An evil wizard has enchanted the magical Beasts of Avantia. Only a true hero can free the Beasts and save the land. Is Tom the hero Avantia has been waiting for?

FERNO
THE FIRE DRAGON
978 1 84616 483 5

SEPRON
THE SEA SERPENT
978 1 84616 482 8

ARCTA
THE MOUNTAIN GIANT
978 1 84616 484 2

TAGUS
THE HORSE-MAN
978 1 84616 486 6

NANOOK
THE SNOW MONSTER
978 1 84616 485 9

EPOS
THE FLAME BIRD
978 1 84616 487 3

DON'T MISS THE
BRAND NEW SERIES OF:

Series 15: VELMAL'S REVENGE

WARDOK
THE SKY TERROR

978 1 40833 487 4

XERIK
THE BONE CRUNCHER

978 1 40833 489 8

PLEXOR
THE RAGING REPTILE

978 1 40833 491 1

QUAGOS
THE ARMOURED BEETLE

978 1 40833 493 5